For Evie, Reilly, Max, and the
entire Solonche family. And especially
to everyone whose name begins with "Al".
—J. F.

To Jamey and to my dogs: Hansel, Gretel, and little
Goblin. Also in memory of Samurai and Jinx,
who are immensely missed.
—E. T.

Published by Two Lions, New York

www.apub.com

Amazon, the Amazon logo, and Two Lions are trademarks of
Amazon.com, Inc., or its affiliates.

ISBN-13: 9781542032438 (hardcover)
ISBN-10: 1542032431 (hardcover)

The illustrations are rendered in digital media.

Book design by AndWorld Design
Printed in China

First Edition
10 9 8 7 6 5 4 3 2 1

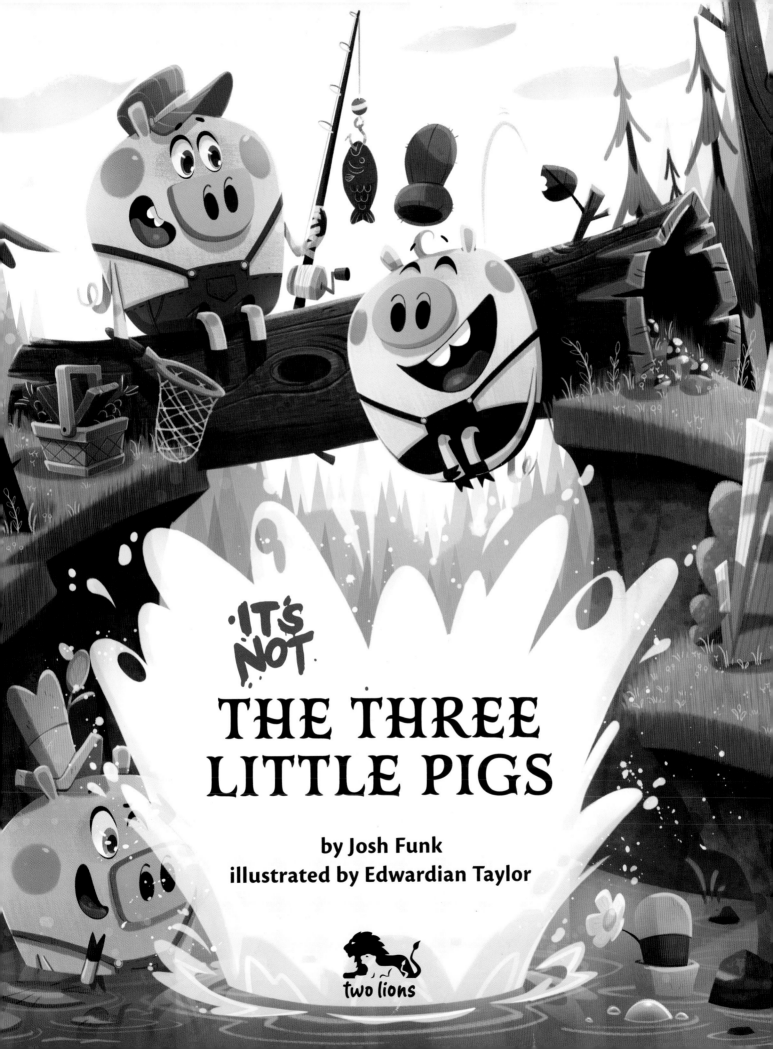

IT'S NOT
THE THREE
LITTLE PIGS

by Josh Funk
illustrated by Edwardian Taylor

two lions

When the young pigs grew old enough, their mother sent them out into the world to seek their fortune.

What does "seek their fortune" mean?

Seeking your fortune means finding your own place to live and getting a job.

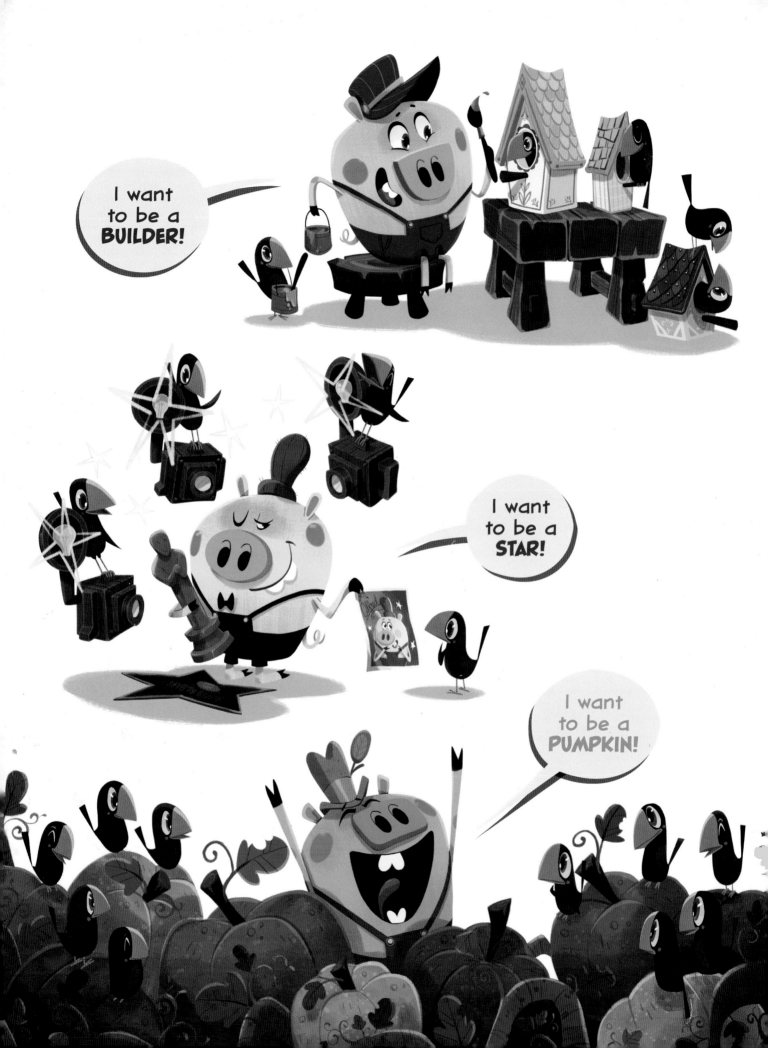

It was a dark and stormy night. The three intrepid pigs began their quest to the magical land of—

NO, NO, NO!

That is not what happened! It started on a warm spring day. And the pigs each went their separate ways.

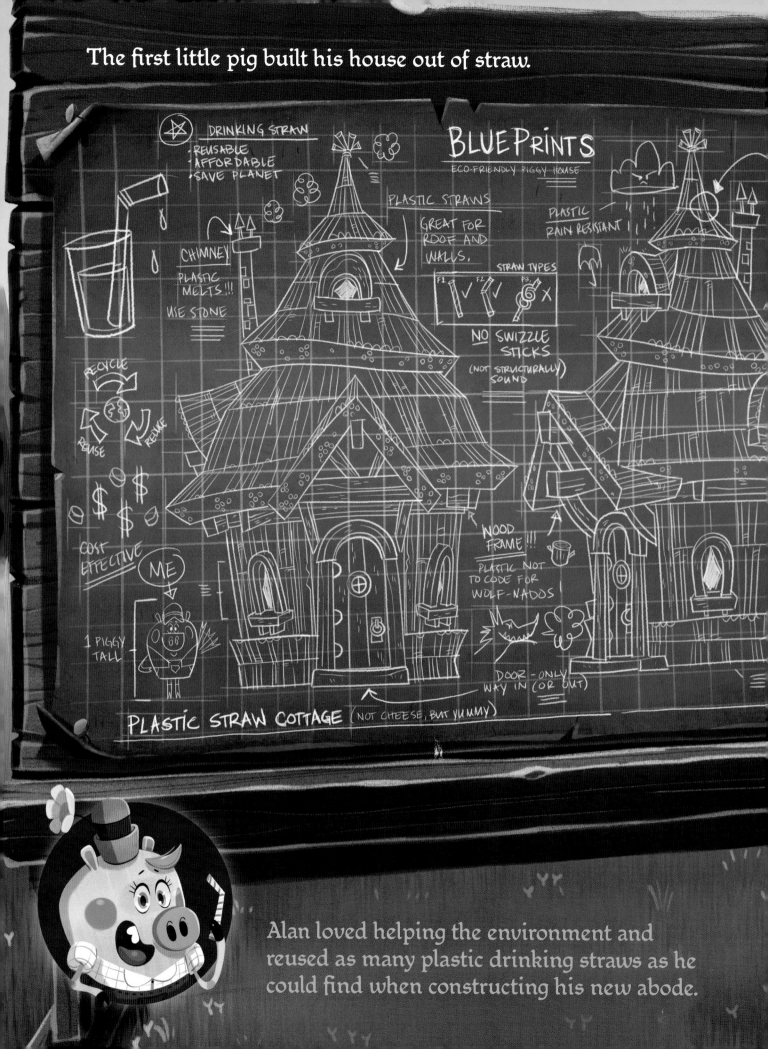

Alan loved helping the environment and reused as many plastic drinking straws as he could find when constructing his new abode.

Just as the house was completed, a hungry wolf approached. He said:

Little pig, little pig, let me come in.

Welcome, friend. Make yourself at—

Don't let the wolf in! He wants to eat you!

Eat me? What do I do?

You're supposed to say, "Not by the hair on my chinny chin chin."

Far too quickly, the pigs arrived at a house made of bricks.

Oh wow! Finally! One of you built your house in advance!

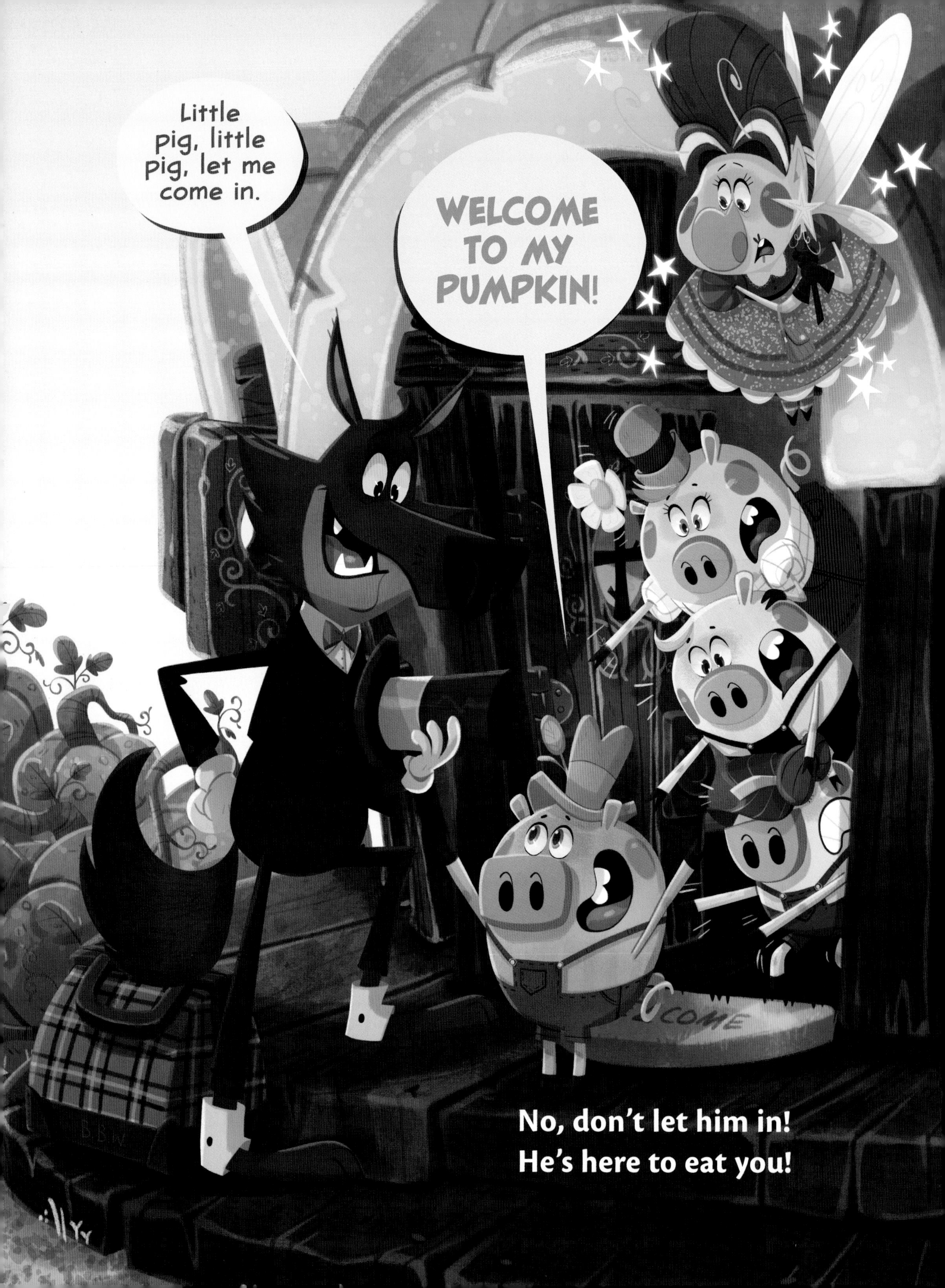

No, don't let him in!
He's here to eat you!

Excuse me. Isn't it possible the story could be better? A little constructive criticism never hurts.

It *did* hurt my feelings a bit.

Look, it's not a terrible starting place.

Thanks . . . ?

But if we work together, we could create a truly amazing story! How does that sound?

I guess that's fair.